Gift to the

from a friend

of the Libray

who wishes

to remain

anonymous

Gift Book Fund

TRAVEL TALES

Ten Fun-Filled Adventures

ABRAMS

...LISHERS

Translated from the French by Toula Ballas
Editor, English-language edition: Nola Butler
Design coordinator, English-language edition: Dana Sloan

Library of Congress Cataloging-in-Publication Data
Travel tales : ten fun-filled adventures / [translated by Toula Ballas].
        p.   cm.
        Contents: I don't want to travel / Emmanuelle Houdart – Zoe's ark / Jacques
Duquennoy – Pipolito / Géraldine Goudard – Ludo and Remi take us for a ride /
Florence Pinel – See you soon, Mr. Pomp! / Lionel le Néouanic – Louise and Pierre go
on a trip / illustrations by Christophe Blain ; story by Marjane Ebrahimi – Aziz, the
blue carpet / Michele Ferri – Alfred of the thousand journeys / Alice Charbin – Going
all around the world, I saw . . . / Joëlle Jolivet – A Snail's Pace / Hélène Riff.
        ISBN 0-8109-3895-2
        1. Travel – Juvenile fiction. 2. Imagination – Juvenile fiction. 3. Children's stories,
French. [1. Travel – Fiction. 2. Imagination – Fiction. 3. Short stories.] I. Ballas, Toula.
        PZ5.T7318   1998
        [Fic] – dc21   98-21103

Copyright © 1998 De La Martinière (Paris, France)
English translation copyright © 1998 Harry N. Abrams, Inc.
Published in 1998 by Harry N. Abrams, Incorporated, New York

Printed and bound in Belgium

Harry N. Abrams, Inc.
100 Fifth Avenue
New York, N.Y. 10011
www.abramsbooks.com

Contents

I DON'T WANT TO TRAVEL

TO

TRAVEL

BY EMMANUELLE HOUDART

EXCEPT IN THE HANDS OF A GIANT

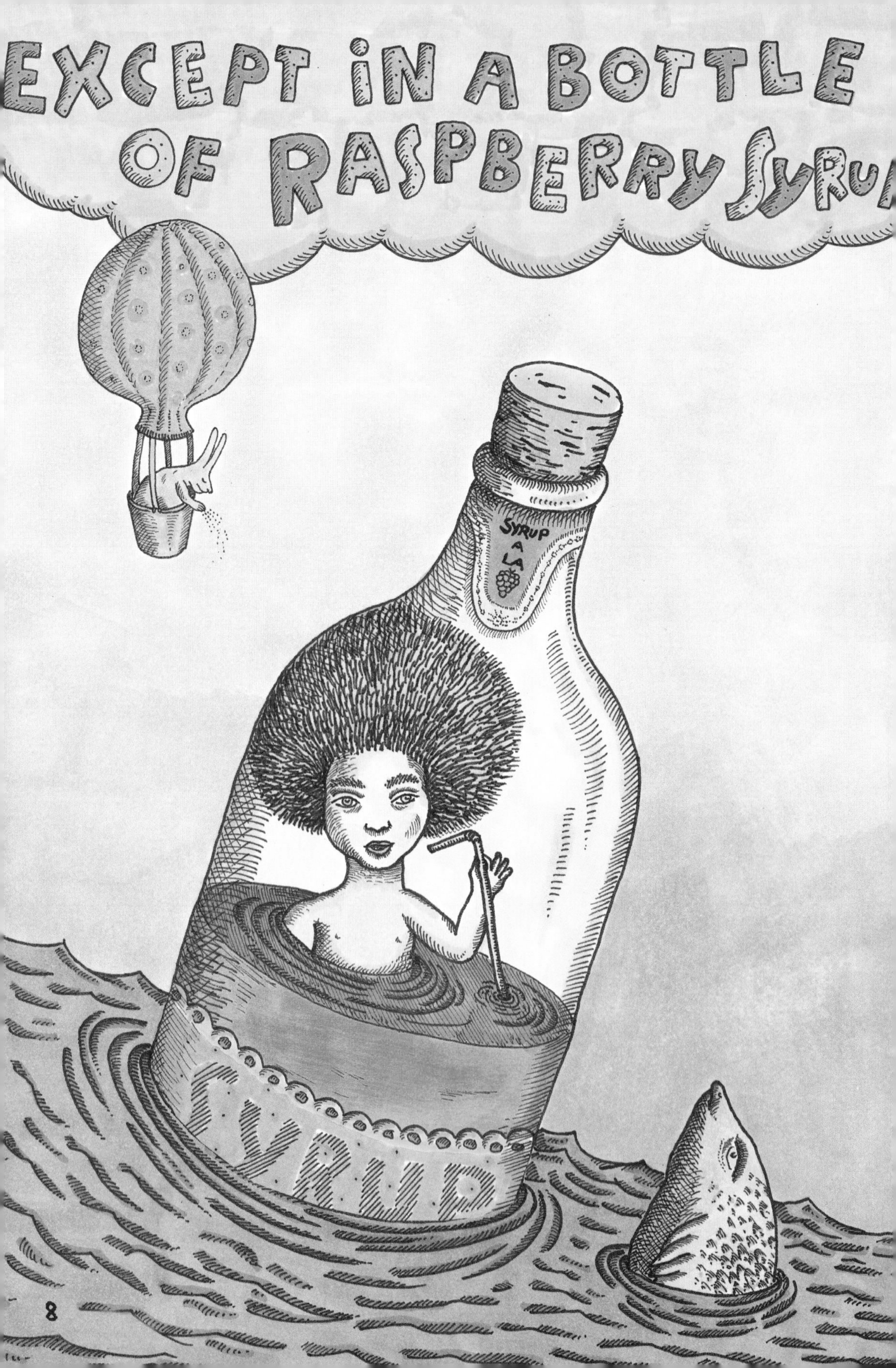

EXCEPT BY THE LIGHT OF THE MOON

11

EXCEPT UNDER THE SEA

ZOE'S ARK

by Jacques Duquennoy

Everybody was bored at the zoo!
Especially Zoe ...

One day, she received
an advertisement in her mailbox:

Zoe didn't hesitate for one second,

she went right down to the pilot school.

There, a wonderful airplane was waiting.

Zoe was a fast learner

and, after several lessons,
she became an excellent pilot.

She knew how to deal with all sorts of
dangerous situations: air pockets, rain,

wind, storms. For the coldest winter days, she even had special attire.

In case of a breakdown, no problem:

Zoe knew how to three-point land
in the middle of a field.

And even how to jump with a parachute!

Now Zoe is able
to pilot a Zooing 747 ...

and everybody's happy!

the end

PIPOLITO

BY GERALDINE GOUDARD

I LIKE TO GO TO BED IN MY FAVORITE PAJAMAS.

WEARING THEM, I CAN TRAVEL ALL NIGHT

ONE TIME, I WAS AT THE NORTH POLE. EVERYTHING WAS

BLUE AND WHITE, BUT I WASN'T EVEN COLD.

THE NEXT NIGHT, I WAS IN THE WILD WEST.

I RODE A BUCKING BRONCO,

EVERYTHING WAS RED

BUT I WASN'T EVEN SCARED

27

Ludo and Remi Take Us for a Ride

by Florence Pinel

Ludo and Remi were great travelers.

I, Ludo, took a plane to visit my uncle.

And, I, Remi, I took a hot-air balloon to the land of giants.

I rode across the Great Plains on horseback.

Well, I crossed the desert on the back of an elephant. 33

In Scotland, I tamed the Loch Ness monster.

On the China Seas, I saved Gong Lee, the whale.

I drove a racing car.

And I, the first solar-powered car.

But it was at the fair that our paths first crossed.

Since then, we have traveled together.

The End

See you soon, Mr. Pomp!

by Lionel Le Néouanic

Mr. Pomp was an odd sort of adventurer.
He never left his house. He was too scared.
Scared of putting on his shoes, scared
that something bad would happen
to him, scared of being scared.
But Mr. Pomp had his own way
of seeing the world without cares:
he traveled in his dreams...

Mr. Pomp always had beautiful dreams and marvelous journeys. He traveled across fantastic landscapes...

and met
incredible people...

42

But one night, horror of horrors!, his beautiful dream turned into a nightmare. Horrible beasts appeared in all directions. Mr. Pomp ran away. But it was in vain, for the monsters trapped him!

MORT E.

Happily, dreams are only dreams, and Mr. Pomp fell back into a deep sleep. Day was breaking. His voyage would soon be over...

Hee hee, I'll see you soon!

The End

Louise and Pierre Go On a Trip

illustrations by **Christophe Blain**
story by **Marjane Ebrahimi**

It's Wednesday, Louise and Pierre are bored.
– What if we went on a trip? shouted Louise.
– A trip? But how? asked Pierre.
– I have an idea. We'll take the red couch and add four wheels, said Louise.
– And wings so it can fly!
– Well . . . why not?
After tinkering for an hour or so, Pierre and Louise settled in and buckled their seat belts.
– Prepare for takeoff! cried Louise.
– No! Wait a second!
– What's the matter?
– I have to pee! said Pierre.

I'm going to drive!

If you start off like that, we'll never get off the ground! said Louise.
Pierre ran off at top speed, then came back and sat next to his sister.
Since Louise was the oldest, she took charge.
(This time, pee or not, we're taking off!)
Vroom! Their airplane lifted off the ground.
– Wow! This is great!

Later, Pierre said:
– Say, Louise . . .
– What now?
– I don't feel so well, he told her, his head hanging over the side.
– Tough luck! We can't go back so soon!
– Aargh!
– Oh, Pierre, you really are disgusting!

The sky grew darker and darker. Louise grew more and more hungry. Pierre, too.
Neither one said a word. They could hardly see. And it was terribly cold so very high up.
Then, the plane started to shake.

An hour passed. Now the sky was completely black.
Poor Pierre and Louise looked straight ahead without seeing a thing.

– Louise? said Pierre.
– What else?
– You're not going to get angry, are you?
– Of course not, go on!
– I'm hungry! said Pierre. I want to go home.

–Fine, OK! grumbled Louise, very hungry herself.
But next time, don't forget the bread and
butter.

The plane began its descent and landed just in time for . . .

"sup

p e r !

AZIZ

THE BLUE CARPET

by Michele Ferri

At Number 2, Merchant's Street, you could find Aziz, the blue carpet, owned by Mr. Bouallak.
Only blue carpets are able to fly, but shhhh!, it's a secret.

Since it was Sunday, Aziz decided to take a little trip.
While Mr. Bouallak had his back turned,
the carpet squeezed under the door without a sound.

In the blink of an eye, Aziz soared toward the sky.
He made some loop-the-loops to loosen up a little,
then he flew over the rooftops.

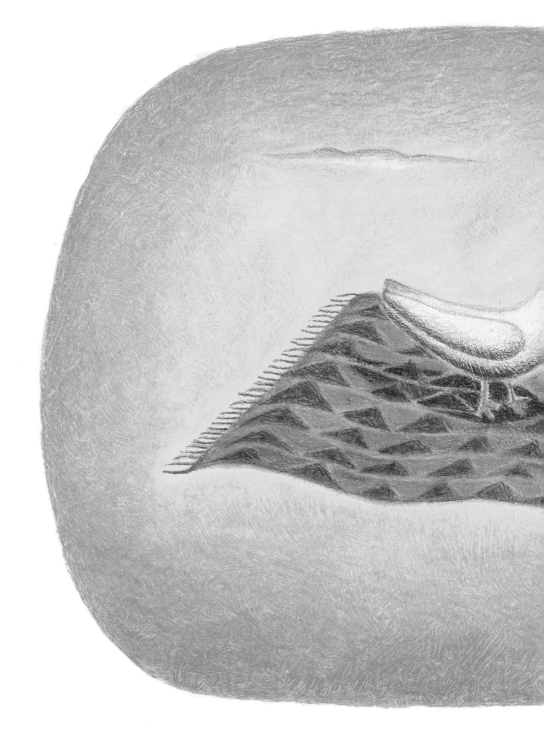

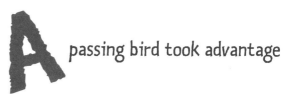

A passing bird took advantage

of the carpet to rest a little.

After having crossed the entire city, Aziz settled on the fourth floor of a big building. This is where Mohammed lived, a very old blue carpet who could hardly fly anymore.

Aziz loved Mohammed's stories. The old carpet told him about his youthful adventures: night flights above the open desert; sandstorms over the dunes; sudden flights of fancy toward the stars; and nosedives at more than 180 mph.

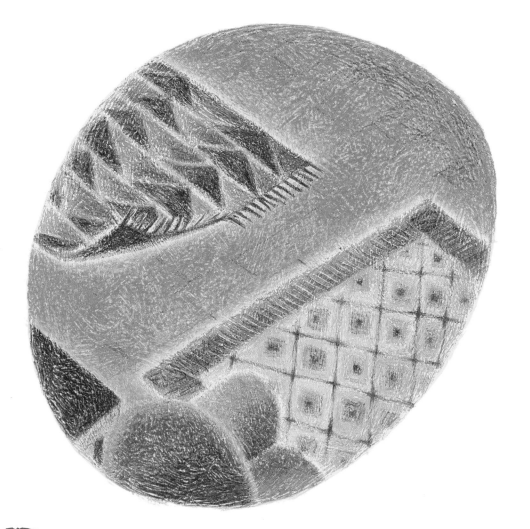

But it was getting late. It was time to go home, thought Aziz, waving his fringes good-bye to Mohammed. Then, he flew out the window, his head full of images.

Aziz flew high in the evening sky, preparing for the great day when he would leave on his own trip to the East.

The end

Alfred of the Thousand Journeys
by Alice Charlie

When I go to my grandmother's, I can travel on a thousand journeys –

I don't even need to take a plane, I just grab my compass and head off in search of abandoned rooms.

I listen to the stories she reads to me. My mind flies away.

I travel between the floors (but not too fast, because it scares me a little...)

The living room is like walking through a strange zoo.

a stuffed weasel

a dangerous fox

a tropical parrot

elephant

a ferocious cat

This is the land of sweets.

BONB

(not like at home where I'm not allowed to eat any)

LAND!

In the garden, I am the discoverer of a new world.

I also explore mysterious underground regions.

67

The garden is a jungle where I battle man-eating animals and carnivorous plants.

Even if it's raining, I can travel in my mind!

On my spirited horse, I take a trip around the world!

And when at last I fall asleep, I start my interstellar journey...

by hélène riff

a snail's pace

'you look like a princess
in your new dress', mama told me.

they've been

talking
and
talking

since the dinner began.

no one's
interested
in a little princess like me.

by the end i was bored.
yes,
me in my new dress,
sitting at the edge
of the table,
bored.
so i made a small
circle with
the leftovers;
zero.
that's it,
i count for

nothing.

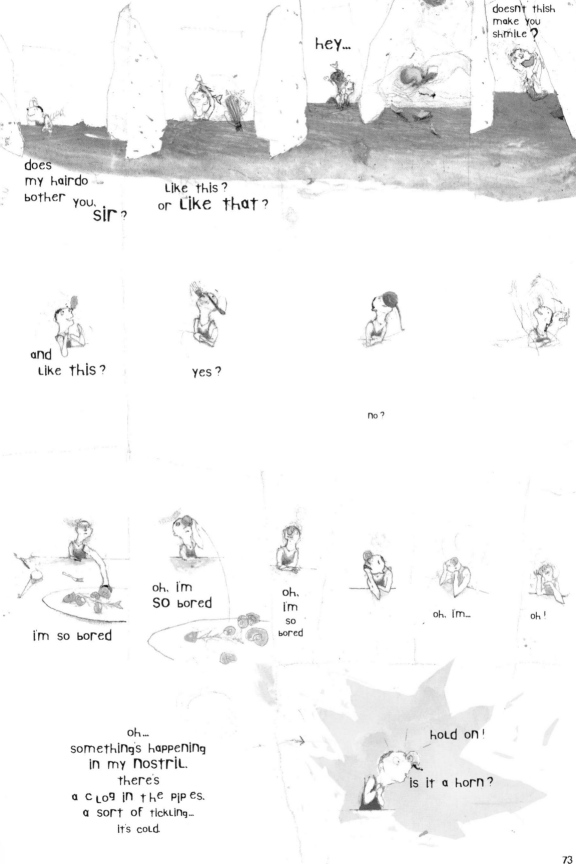

in the name of the snail!

that's it!

that's my nose, my little nose crawling across the tablecloth.

my nose is sailing across the big white sea, it's gliding.

oh...

oh...

oh, my goodness!

12

i can sense every head turning, oh, they're turning

oh...

"in the name of the pumpkin!" cried out mama. "it's almost midnight!"

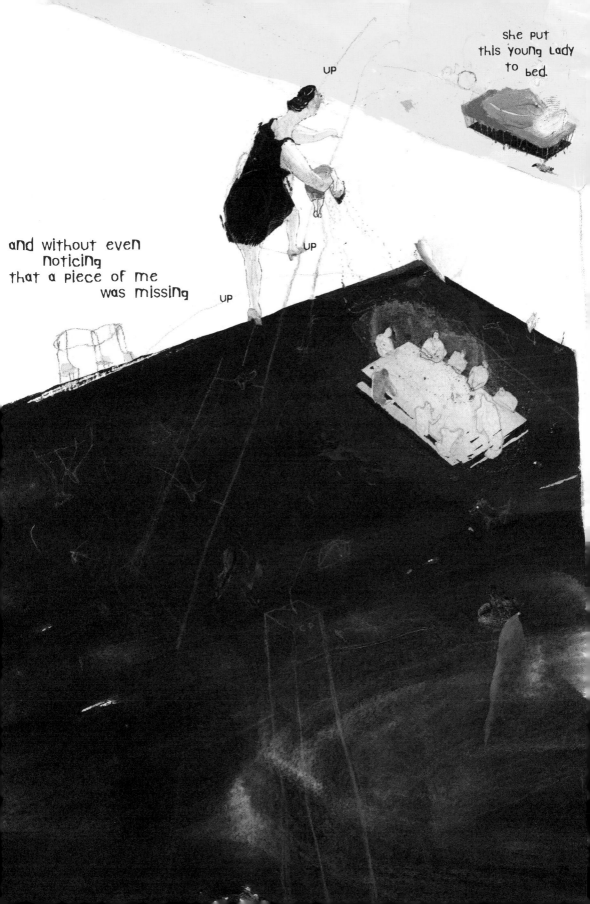

now,

i am truly a princess because without leaving my bed i can travel

12 hold on, what's
glistening inside?
is it salt?

13 and tha
could th

11 and look up there,
two flies circling,
black on black

10 in the name
of the dog!

9 thump,
thump,
thump

8 tick, tock,
tick, tock

7 a tender
caress,
pat, pat

where i want to and   feel,
              feel, feel,   ...
                    1 up into the hills,
                       down into the gardens

e pep... pep.. ah ah ah ah
                    ah
                    2 to hear a sweet voice

                    3 my goodness! what smells?

                    4 across the rough,
                       rough sea of the tablecloth
                          (im almost over the edge!)

    6 look how   5 to slip through
       the night   the grass on the
    sparkles!   nape of a neck

ah

...choo !

b

and there it is. i have smelled
the sweetest
of smells.
the warm palm
of mama's hand,
come especially
to put back
in its place
_ just between
the forehead
and the mouth _
my little button
with two holes
in it.

.......ess you' said mama

(mama understands
everything at once)